The Runaway Pumpkin

by **Kevin Lewis**

illustrated by **S. D. Schindler**

ORCHARD BOOKS
An imprint of Scholastic Inc. • New York

Once upon a hill,
when the wind blew with a chill

wandered Buck and Billy Baxter
with their baby sister, Lil.

And there, upon that hillside,
growing orange, fat, and fine
the budding Baxters found a pumpkin
on a twisty, twirly vine.

It was big and it was round,
and the boys, their eyes a-gleam,
gave a whoop, a yell, a holler
no finer pumpkin had they seen.

And today was Halloween.

Yet little Lil was cautious,
    and, of course, she tried to warn them,
        but her bumbling, big-head brothers
            snapped the pumpkin from its stem.

            And as she watched them roll it,
                at first real slow, but then much faster,
                    little Lil looked down the hill
                        and she foresaw disaster!

'Round and 'round
across the ground
makin' a
thumpin'
bumpin' sound

came that

thumpety

bumpety

thumpin'

bumpin'
round and roll-y
RUNAWAY PUMPKIN!

A short way down the hillside,
that zooming pumpkin caught the eye
of mucking Momma Baxter,
who thought of Granny's pumpkin pie

'til it **BUSTED** through her sty!

'Round and 'round
across the ground
makin' a
thumpin'
bumpin' sound
came that
thumpety,
bumpety
thumpin'
bumpin'
round and roll-y
RUNAWAY PUMPKIN!

A bit farther down the hillside,
just beyond the chicken coop,
Grampa Baxter saw that pumpkin
and thought of Granny's pumpkin soup

'til it KNOCKED him for a loop!

'Round and 'round
across the ground
makin' a
thumpin'
bumpin' sound
came that
thumpety
bumpety
thumpin'
bumpin'
round and roll-y
RUNAWAY PUMPKIN!

Now, at the bottom of that hillside,
where that boundin' pumpkin sped,
Poppa Baxter on his tractor
thought of Granny's pumpkin bread

but Poppa Baxter used his head
and quickly plowed a pumpkin bed!

So at the bottom of the hillside,
   fat and round upon the ground,
      that thumpin', bumpin' pumpkin plopped
         and didn't make another sound.

And as pigs and hens and Baxters
gathered 'round where Poppa plowed
little Lil, she gathered Granny
and pulled her through the waiting crowd.

Buck and Billy looked really proud.

Then thumpety
bumpety
thumpin'
bumpin'
straight to the kitchen
went that pumpkin.

And soon after came the smell
of dear old Granny cookin' somethin'.

Granny stirred and stewed and baked
until the bright full moon rose up
and all those hungry Baxters
sat themselves right down to sup.

And at the center of the table,
among the soup and bread and pie,

For Ilana, Bella, Emma, Hannah, Grace,
and all girls who are on a roll! — K. L.

Text
copyright
© 2003 by
Kevin Lewis •
Illustrations copyright
© 2003 by S. D. Schindler •
All rights reserved. Published by
Orchard Books, an imprint of Scholastic
Inc. ORCHARD BOOKS and design are registered
trademarks of Watts Publishing Group, Ltd., used
under license. SCHOLASTIC and associated logos are trademarks
and/or registered trademarks of Scholastic Inc. No part of this publication
may be reproduced, or stored in a retrieval system, or transmitted in any form
or by any means, electronic, mechanical, photocopying, recording, or otherwise,
without written permission of the publisher. For information regarding permission,
write to Orchard Books, Scholastic Inc., Permissions Department, 557 Broadway, New
York, NY 10012. • LIBRARY OF CONGRESS CATALOGING-IN-PUBLICATION DATA AVAILABLE • ISBN: 0-439-
43974-4 • 10 9 8 7 6 5 4 3 2 1   03 04 05 06 07 • Reinforced binding for Library
Use • Printed in Singapore 46 • First Scholastic edition, September 2003 • Book design by David Caplan
The text type was set in SpleenyDecafGD. The title type was hand lettered by David Coulson.